I Love You,
Blue Kangaroo!

Emma Chichester Clark

Dragonfly Books® New York

for
Lily Brown
and her little brother
Jack

Published by
Dragonfly Books®
an imprint of
Random House Children's Books
a division of Random House, Inc.
1540 Broadway
New York, New York 10036

Copyright © 1998 by Emma Chichester Clark
First American edition 1999
First published in Great Britain by Andersen Press Ltd., 1998

Visit us on the Web! www.randomhouse.com/kids

Educators and librarians, for a variety of teaching tools, visit us at www.randomhouse.com/teachers

ISBN: 0-385-32638-6 (trade)   0-440-41549-7 (pbk.)
The text of this book is set in 20-point Garamond.
Reprinted by arrangement with Doubleday Books for Young Readers
Printed in the United States of America
January 2001
10 9 8 7 6 5 4 3 2 1

Blue Kangaroo belonged to Lily.
He was her very own kangaroo.
Every night, Lily said,
"I love you, Blue Kangaroo!"
And Blue Kangaroo fell fast asleep in Lily's arms.

Then one day, Lily's aunt Jemima came for lunch.
She gave Lily a wild brown bear.

He was huggable and furry, with wild brown eyes.

That night, Lily took the wild brown bear
up to bed with her. She said,
"I love Wild Brown Bear . . .

". . . and I love you, Blue Kangaroo!"

Blue Kangaroo
didn't sleep quite
so well after that.

The next Saturday, Lily's mother's friend Florence
came to tea. She gave Lily a yellow cotton rabbit.

He was floppy and fleecy, with velvety ears.

That night, as Lily got ready for bed, she said,
"I love Yellow Cotton Rabbit . . .

. . . I love Wild Brown Bear,
and I love you, Blue Kangaroo!"

Blue Kangaroo
hardly slept at all
after that.

Then jolly Uncle George came to stay.
He gave Lily two furry puppies.

They were cuddly and fluffy, with shiny black noses.

That night, as Lily put her pajamas on, she said,
"I love the Furry Puppies . . .

. . . I love Yellow Cotton Rabbit,
I love Wild Brown Bear,
and I love you, Blue Kangaroo!"

After that,
Blue Kangaroo
hardly slept a wink.

On Lily's birthday, Mrs. Appleby gave Lily
a wiggly green crocodile, and her great-uncle Arthur

gave her a long-eared owl.
Lily's cousin, Amelia, gave her a little tiny teddy.

That night, as Lily brushed her teeth, she said,
"I love Tiny Teddy, I love Long-Eared Owl,
I love Wiggly Green Crocodile . . .

. . . I love the Furry Puppies,
I love Yellow Cotton Rabbit,
I love Wild Brown Bear,
and I love you, Blue Kangaroo!"

Blue Kangaroo lay on
the edge of the bed
and stared at the ceiling.

In the middle of the night, Lily rolled over.
Then Tiny Teddy rolled over.
Then Long-Eared Owl rolled over.
Then Wiggly Green Crocodile rolled over.

Then the Furry Puppies rolled over.
Then Yellow Cotton Rabbit rolled over.
Then Wild Brown Bear rolled over . . .

. . . and Blue Kangaroo rolled out of bed, onto the floor.
He looked up at Lily and the sleeping creatures.

"There's just no room for me anymore," he said sadly,
and he hopped across the carpet and out the door.

He hopped along the hallway
to the baby's room,
and he hopped up
into the baby's warm crib.

"Goo goo, boo gangaloo!"
gurgled the baby
as he squeezed Blue Kangaroo
tightly in his little pink fists.

The next day, Lily looked everywhere
for Blue Kangaroo.
"Goo goo, boo gangaloo!" cooed the baby.

"Mine!" cried the baby.
"No!" shouted Lily.

"Lily!" said her mother. "You've got so many animals.
Surely you can let the baby have just one?"
"Not Blue Kangaroo!" cried Lily.

Lily ran to her room and when she came back,
her arms were full.
"He can have all of these," she said,
"but nobody can have Blue Kangaroo!"

That night, the baby went to bed with
the wild brown bear, the yellow cotton rabbit,
the furry puppies, the wiggly green crocodile,
the long-eared owl, and the little tiny teddy.

Lily went to bed with Blue Kangaroo.
Blue Kangaroo snuggled up to Lily. She stroked his
blue ears; then she kissed the tip of his soft blue nose.
"I love you, Blue Kangaroo!" she said . . .

. . . and Blue Kangaroo
fell fast asleep
in her arms.